A DINNER TO DIE FOR

A DANIEL HANNITY MYSTERY

MICHAEL RYDER

THOMAS PUBLISHING

COPYRIGHT

Sign up for Michael Ryder's email newsletter

Get an email update when a new Michael Ryder book is ready. You can unsubscribe at any time with one click.

<u>Sign up at AuthorMichaelRyder.com</u>

In honor of Rex Stout

CHAPTER
ONE

BARRY and I were in our usual spots in the back, nursing whiskeys and arguing the finer points of the 49ers' latest screwup, when my attention was drawn to a flash of light and movement up front. A gorgeous gal had walked into the bar and approached Jimmy, owner of this fine establishment. "Excuse me," we heard her say. "I'm looking for Daniel Hannity."

Jimmy, bless his crusty Irish heart, said something in his quiet low voice and pointed her our way.

The gal swiveled toward us and I adjusted my spectacles to enjoy the view. Heck, I may be old as dust, but this woman was worth the effort. From the neck up she was an angel — short blond hair, big blue eyes, dimpled chin. But from the neck down, in her chic black leather jacket, black sweater, black jeans, and black leather high-heel boots that you know cost a fortune, she came across as a tempting mix of class and va-va-voom. She looked confident and smart and aware of her beauty — the kind of woman who knew what she wanted and knew how to get it.

Except maybe that day. That day, alone in a rundown Irish bar in the lower Mission on the left side of noon on a Tuesday, she looked uncertain and out of place. I knew what she was thinking: Why would Daniel Hannity hang out here? Was San Francisco's best private detective some kind of drunk?

She thanked Jimmy and strode toward me and Barry, assessing us in turn as she tried to figure out through the bar's dim light if one of us was Danny.

Me, she dismissed with a single glance — no way the skinny white guy with the big glasses and mad-scientist hair, wearing a "Fight the Power" t-shirt, was Daniel Hannity. Quite right, too, since my name is Jake Sears and I'm about a thousand years older and a million times more agreeable than the kid in question.

Her eyes lingered a second longer on Barry before dismissing him as well. Barry was my age but hid it better. He was big and Black and solid, with watchful eyes and a reserved demeanor, dressed in a brown pullover sweater over a collared shirt. It was only when she got close enough to see the gray in his hair that her walk faltered.

"Excuse me," she said. "I'm looking for Daniel Hannity."

"He's not here," I said, "but I'm his confidential assistant."

That was a joke, of course — Danny isn't my employer and I'm nobody's assistant, thank you very much — but I get a kick out of saying it, especially to the younger generation. The phrase has an aura. It throws people off-balance, opens them up a crack, gives me a glimpse of what they're really about.

The gorgeous gal didn't know to make of me, but she was sharp enough to sense I might be playing her.

"Is that so?" she said, her tone noncommittal. "Can you tell me where he is?"

"I might," I said. "Miss...?"

"My name is Claire Hawthorne."

That's when the gears snapped into place. Next to me, I heard Barry's spine crackle. I wanted to kick myself for not recognizing her sooner. I was gonna need something stronger than whiskey to soothe the knot that popped from out of nowhere in my stomach.

Barry and I knew who Claire Hawthorne was. Everyone in San Francisco knew who the lovely young wife — now widow — of rich old Harold Hawthorne was. When Harold married her a year back, he'd just turned eighty and had been a fixture on the social scene for decades — the epitome of old San Francisco money. Claire, in contrast, was his opposite in every way: twenty-eight and beautiful, a nobody from nowhere, a would-be interior designer working odd jobs to pay the rent.

The media, of course, quickly did the math and, loving how it added up, dished everything they could about the noteworthy couple. How they met at a fancy-schmancy event where Claire worked as a cater-waiter. How Harold wooed her with getaways to Paris and Hong Kong. How the mayor, an old friend of Harold's, officiated their nuptials. How Claire, dressed in the latest fashions, wowed the swells at the big society events. And how Harold's son and daughter — both older than their new stepmom — were furious when Harold announced he was putting most of his wealth into his charitable foundation, with Claire in charge.

Fast-forward to four weeks ago, when Harold

Hawthorne died after eleven months of wedded bliss. At first, the word was he passed after a bout of food poisoning. But it wasn't long before rumors of a non-accidental sort started flying. Had Harold — by all accounts a notorious old goat — tired of his new wife and decided to trade her in? Had the lovely Claire, concerned about her hubby's continued vitality, nudged him toward his eternal slumber before he could kick her to the curb? Harold's children had no qualms about fanning the flames, insinuating to the press (through anonymous "family friends," of course) that Claire had been more than a cater-waiter when she met Harold — that she'd been in the business of offering hospitality of the second-oldest sort. When the police announced they were opening an active homicide investigation, the story went into overdrive.

Now, about the knot in my stomach. Barry and I exchanged a look, and Barry nodded.

"Mrs. Hawthorne," I said. "My name is Jake Sears and this big galoot is Barry Rawlins. We served with your dad Carl in Vietnam."

Her eyes widened. Whatever she'd been expecting, it wasn't that.

"Before your dad died, he asked us to help you out if you needed it."

"My dad...." she said, her eyes darting from me to Barry and back.

"We saw him about a year ago, at a reunion of our unit. To be honest, he wasn't looking too good. He told us about the lung cancer. And then he said his daughter Claire was in San Francisco. He was worried about her. She was marrying a guy and he didn't like the guy's family. So he said, 'Can you keep an eye out? Help her if she needs it?'"

Claire's eyes filled with emotion.

I continued. "I don't like vague requests and neither does Barry, but what could we say? Your dad was there for us, back in the day. We owed him. So we said sure, we'd keep an eye out."

Barry spoke up then, his voice as deep and resonant as you'd expect. "Your father was a good man, Mrs. Hawthorne. Our condolences for your loss."

She started to say something, then stopped. She took a deep breath and blinked rapidly, trying to hold back tears. That was the moment I started liking her — when I saw how much she hated the situation she found herself in, and not just because she was in serious legal jeopardy. This gal needed help and wasn't copacetic about that. The lovely Claire Hawthorne was as independent-minded as yours truly.

I looked again at Barry, the question unspoken but obvious, and he nodded in agreement.

I turned back to Claire. "About Daniel Hannity. Here's what we're gonna do. Barry's gonna text the Boy Wonder."

I stood up from my stool. "And I'm going to take you to him."

CHAPTER
TWO

TO BE CLEAR, Danny's no Boy Wonder, at least not anymore. He's thirty-four now, big and wide enough to be a defensive tackle. But I've always thought of him as a kid and I guess I always will. His dad Jimmy and Barry and I go way back — Vietnam, cobwebs stuff, not the point of this tale — which means I've known Danny since he was a mewling babe, screaming and fussing in his mama's arms. When he got older, when he earned comic book money by helping his dad clean the bar to get it ready for another night of booze-slinging, he got in the habit of testing his knowledge on me. He liked to read, and he liked to challenge and push. Which made me a perfect foil, because as anyone will tell you, I tell it like it is and don't hold back.

Like one day, after mopping down half the floor, he comes to me and says, "I read that JFK was assassinated by the CIA because he decided to not escalate the war in Vietnam." The kid was eleven and big for his age. At first glance, with his blond hair and broad face, he looked kind of stupid, like he was destined for the role of doltish sidekick who laughed when his smaller pal cracked a joke.

It was only when you looked past his size, when you saw those penetrating grey eyes, that you realized you were dealing with something different.

"Way out of your league, kid." I could have lied — should have, given the topic — but like I said, I tell it like it is.

He didn't say anything, just grinned, knowing he'd learned something, then turned to finish his mopping. He'd already figured out, through certain conversations he might have overheard in which I might have said too much after imbibing a bit too much of my favorite liquid refreshment, that I might have firsthand experience with a certain organization riddled with elitist jerks who think they're entitled to run the world. And by experience, let's just say, for the sake of hypothetical argument, I might have a talent for making fake stuff look real and vice-versa. Which means I might get hired every now and again by same said unnamed organization to make illegitimate documents look legit, or to disguise valuable objects so they can cross borders without incident.

And let me say that, while I had no direct knowledge of what the kid asked about, I'd pieced together enough random tidbits over the years to wonder if his thesis might be right.

But I wasn't gonna tell the kid that. If I had, he would have run with it. He would have gone to the papers, written his congressman, done his idealistic best to make a difference. He was still a kid at that point — he had yet to learn that the world rewards people who play along. He had yet to realize that activists and reformers, even when they buck the odds and succeed, too often pay a heavy price.

While Barry used his big fingers to text a message to Danny, I used my phone to order a cab, then got up from my stool and shrugged into my sports jacket. With a nod to Jimmy, I escorted the lovely Claire out of the bar.

She looked me over while we waited outside, trying to get a handle. I know I'm not much to look at — I'm skinnier and shorter than I prefer — but I like to think I make up for that with attitude.

"About Danny," I said to her. "He's like a barnacle. Tough to pry loose. No guarantees, okay?"

She nodded. "Where are we going?"

"His place." I scanned the block — no cab yet. "While we're waiting, mind if I ask how you knew to come to Jimmy's?"

"A friend is a former client. She told me."

"What else do you know about Danny?"

"What my friend told me, and what I found when I searched."

Which meant she knew the basics. She knew that two years ago Danny had been the youngest homicide inspector in SFPD history, and that after he cracked a bunch of high-profile cases, the brass and the media conspired to turn him into a poster boy. She knew that, two years ago, he was newly married to his college sweetheart Natalie and about to move into a beautiful Victorian that Natalie bought and meticulously restored (with her startup millions) on a hill overlooking Dolores Park.

And she knew that Danny's fairy tale ended the morning he and Natalie got broadsided by a truck on their way to Napa for a wine weekend, killing Natalie and badly injuring Danny. And she probably knew that after retiring from the force and enduring multiple leg and knee surgeries, Danny pretty much disappeared into the big empty Victorian on the hill, pushing the world away while he lost himself in wine and whiskey and video games.

What Claire probably didn't know is that those of us who knew him best — his mom and dad and brother, along with me and Barry — put up with his hermit routine for a good long while. We let him be, let him stew in his own juices, tried to give him the space and time he needed.

For a year, that is. Then we got impatient. Hence my new part-time job: poking the bear. It's a tough gig, no denying, but one I'm good at. I think of myself as the sand in his oyster, the mosquito buzzing in his ear, the cattle prod in his backside. Or, in this particular instance, the dangler of cases to which the former Boy Wonder Would Not Be Allowed to Say No. Basically, if a lever existed to pry the kid out of his house and force him into face-to-face interactions with other human beings, I was open to yanking it. I wasn't always successful — usually he just growled and snarled and turned away — but every now and then he bit. He'd taken on a half-dozen cases as a private investigator in the past year. He'd even, to my amazement, joined me and Barry a few times — voluntarily! — for cards in the back room of his dad's bar.

All such recent progress aside, I knew that bringing a potential client to the inner sanctum was risky. The maneuver would be interpreted as an invasion of the den: an intrusion, an escalation, even an outrage. But given the circumstances, the move felt necessary. The lovely Claire was time-challenged. The cops had her in their sights. An arrest might come any moment. If Danny was going to take her case, he was going to have to take it now, as in today.

The cab pulled up and we slid in. A couple of minutes passed in silence as the city rushed by. Every now and then, probably without realizing it, Claire clenched her fists. When the cab hit the steep blocks that rose from the Mission, she snapped out of her zone. "Sorry. I get stress headaches."

"We're almost there. And remember, I do the talking."

The cab pulled over and we stepped out in front of a grand old Victorian. It was a beauty of a house, built in 1892, a lucky survivor of the 1906 quake and fire. Three stories of Painted Lady charm, decked out in a vibrant mix of blue, gray, red, cream and gold.

We walked up the steps to the front door. I rang the doorbell, waited fifteen seconds for Danny to make himself presentable, then slid my key into the lock and pushed open the door. After ushering Claire into the entry foyer, I closed the door behind us and led her into the living room.

The room was beautiful — spacious and generously proportioned, with a high ceiling, dark hardwood floors, and tall bay windows. Or at least it would have been, were its beauty not besmirched by the big unsightly mess in the middle of it. As expected, the former Boy Wonder was planted like a grumpy lump on his big brown couch, unshaven and unshowered in his usual Stanford sweatshirt and cargo shorts. An empty pizza box lay on the coffee table in front of him, next to an empty bottle of wine and his cane. With his hands, he was manipulating a game controller to make the big tough soldier on the big flat-screen TV on the wall shoot his big gun and hide behind wrecked cars while bullets whizzed by.

Aside from the physical objects I just described, the living room was empty. As in, bare bones. As in, no pictures or lamps or chairs or rug. As in, Danny hadn't done a damn thing to decorate. As in, he'd lugged in a couch and a coffee table and a way-too-big TV up the stairs and through the front door of his beautiful empty Victorian home and then done exactly nothing else to make the place livable. He was like a college kid on his first day in the dorm, or a homeless squatter in an abandoned building.

He glanced our way and frowned when he saw I'd brought a visitor.

"No," he said, then turned back to the screen.

Next to me, Claire looked ready to bolt. I couldn't blame her. She was getting a full dose of Danny in all of his unvarnished glory — a grown man playing a stupid video game on a Tuesday afternoon like a depressed unemployed loser.

"Snap to it, kid," I said. "Mrs. Claire Hawthorne's got a problem with your name written all over it."

For a few long seconds, he gave us nothing. Then he sighed and hit the pause button. The big soldier on the big TV froze in mid-leap.

He swiveled to face us, his eyes moving from me to Claire.

"Mrs. Hawthorne," he said, "you'll have to forgive Jake. Sometimes he forgets he's not my boss."

"Are you the Daniel Hannity who helped Emily Burnham?" Claire said.

She'd tried to maintain a polite tone when she said it, but it was clear she had her doubts.

Danny didn't blink. Now, if you were a normal person and found yourself in a situation in which strangers were looking at you and judging you because you were dressed like a slobby slacker and you knew you were grossing them out, you'd do something about it. You'd run your hands over your hair, tuck in your shirt, maybe apologize for your appearance. You'd do something to acknowledge the validity of their point of view. You'd do that because you're normal and that's what normal people do.

Danny's not like that. More than anyone I've ever met, he truly doesn't care what most people think about him. He cared what Natalie thought about him, of course, and he cares what his mom and dad and brother think about him, up to a point. Sometimes he even cares what Barry and I think about him. But the rest of the world can stuff it.

Before he demonstrated his lack of caring by telling us to get the hell out of his house, I jumped in. "Claire is the daughter of an old buddy."

His grey eyes flickered back to me. "Vietnam?"

"Yeah," I said, holding his gaze.

His lips tightened. He understood then that I was calling in a favor, of which he owes me several hundred.

He closed his eyes and went still for a few seconds, then put down the video controller, inched forward on the couch, grabbed the cane he uses to keep his weight off his knee, and stood up. He's a big guy, with extra pounds around the middle he needs to get rid of, so the displacement of mass upward from couch to standing position was truly a sight to behold.

He shook his bad leg to stretch it, then slowly settled his weight and turned to face us. "I'm aware of your predicament, Mrs. Hawthorne. It's hard not to be." He aimed his eyes at her. "Did you kill your husband?"

Her nostrils flared. A flush rose on her cheeks but she didn't flinch. "No," she said, holding his gaze. "My turn. What would your dead wife say about" — she gestured toward the couch — "this?"

His eyes narrowed.

"I loved my husband, Mr. Hannity," she said, lip trembling. "Just as I'm sure you loved your wife."

"Why are you here?"

"Because you were recommended. Because I'm in trouble. Because your friend Jake brought me."

"What do you want from me?"

"I want you to find out who killed my husband."

He didn't move a muscle. His eyes didn't leave her face. He stood there like a block of concrete and let his brain and gut tell him what to do. This moment always happened. When it did, his body went into statue mode. One time I watched him stand perfectly still for three full minutes while he diverted blood to his brain and let it work. Except for an occasional eye blink, he didn't move a muscle. If that doesn't sound weird, try it yourself sometime. Try it when people are looking at you and waiting for an answer. Trust me, it's weird.

If I hadn't already pulled an obligation chit out of my pocket and waved it in his face, I know he would have declined the case. That was his default response. If a case or a client bored him, he declined the case. If he was in the middle of a stupid action sequence in one of his stupid video games, he declined the case. If the sky was blue or gray or clear or foggy, if the sun was shining or the moon was out, if the wind was coming from the west or east or north or south or wasn't there at all, if the day of the week ended in "day," he declined the case.

My chit meant his usual anti-social default option would not suffice. He knew he only had one out I'd accept as legit: If he thought a would-be client was guilty, he declined the case.

So what was Danny's famous gut telling him about the lovely Claire? And what, for that matter, was my gut — and I had a pretty good one, if I do say so — telling me?

It turns out they were telling us the same thing.

The kid sighed, threw me a baleful look, then turned back to Claire. "Mrs. Hawthorne, I'll take your case."

CHAPTER
THREE

AH, the sweet smell of victory. Or rather, the not-so-faint aroma of unwashed Danny and his overused brown couch.

"Not here, kid," I said to him. "We'll talk in the back room. You clean up and meet us in forty-five."

He didn't argue. From the look of it, he'd been up most of the night with that stupid game, drinking wine and whiskey and blasting bad guys, so he knew he stank. Plus, he didn't have chairs for guests and hated being reminded of that inconvenient truth, because what usually followed the surfacing of said truth was someone asking him why he didn't do something about it, and there was no way for him to answer that question without acknowledging the possibility — no, let me rephrase, the *horror* — that someday he might actually choose to welcome guests into his home again and engage the world again and start living this strange and painful and wonderful thing called life again.

I turned to Danny's new client. "Okay, let's go."

She blinked, startled. "Go?"

"Back to Jimmy's." I pulled out my phone, ordered us a cab, then ushered us out of the house and to the curb.

Claire gave me a quizzical look. "Why did he agree to take my case?"

"Because he decided you're innocent."

"I am innocent."

"Good, we all agree. The hard part will be proving it."

At the bottom of the hill, a cab turned the corner and plowed up the hill, its engine revving as it inched up the steep incline. When the guy reached us, we climbed in and hurtled back toward the bar.

I texted Barry. "In. Back room."

I haven't described the back room at Jimmy's yet, so let me set the scene. For years, Jimmy used it as a storage space. Then one day Enrique, the head waiter at Fiorello's, the Italian restaurant next door, had an idea. "Your back room, let's fix it up, rent it out for private dinners. You do the liquor, we do the food." Jimmy liked the idea and before we could blink, he and Fiorello and Enrique knocked a door in the wall between the bar and the restaurant and spiffed the space up. The room looked like a private club now, with a big Persian rug over a hardwood floor, and redwood paneling, grey-blue wallpaper, and framed photos of old San Francisco on the walls.

Most of the time, the room was set up with a dining table in the center of the room with seating for twenty. On poker nights, we pulled chairs around a single table. When Danny started taking private cases, he got in the habit of using the room for meetings, an arrangement that suited everyone — Jimmy because it got his son out of his house, Danny because it kept clients away from his house, and Barry and I because it kept us close to our favorite barstools.

I was up at the front of the bar, giving Jimmy the lay of the land, when Danny and his cane limped in. He was freshly showered and shaved, in his usual jeans, button-down shirt, and comfortable walking shoes.

The kid gave his dad a nod. Jimmy nodded back — big talkers, the two of them — then gestured toward the back room, where Claire and Barry were cooling their heels. "You sure about this one?"

"Reasonably," Danny said.

Jimmy picked up a bottle of whiskey, set a shot glass on the bar, and poured. Like the rest of us, he'd been following the news, so he knew the lovely Claire was in serious trouble. Understandably, he was concerned about his son choosing to stand in front of the legal freight train hurtling her way. But verbal exposition wasn't Jimmy's style, so instead he let his fatherly concern flow into the glass.

Danny brought the whiskey to his lips. "I'll be careful, promise." He turned and headed to the back room, me a step behind. When he got there, he looked at the setup — four chairs, arranged in a circle in the center of the room — and settled into the biggest one, a big wide worn leather wingback chair that best accommodated his bulk. Barry and I sat in the chairs on either side of him, leaving the chair opposite for his new client.

You might be wondering at this point: Why no table? The choice was Danny's. When he met with people on a case, he liked to arrange the chairs in a close circle with nothing in-between. He liked looking at people from head to toe to catch any clues he could from body language.

Claire frowned at the setup, but only for a second. She set her handbag on the floor and sat down, crossing one long leg over the other. Unlike most first-timers to Danny's circles, she didn't try to fill the nervous silence with talk. She watched and waited while Danny set his cane on the floor and stretched his bad leg out in front of him.

He held her gaze for a few long seconds.

"Mrs. Hawthorne," he said.

"Please," she said, "call me Claire."

He shook his head. "Not as long you're my client. I prefer to think in formal terms when considering a case."

Her eyebrows rose — her homework on him hadn't included that — but she let it pass. "All right, Mr. Hannity."

He nodded. "We — and by we I mean Mr. Rawlins and Mr. Sears and myself — know only the broad brushstrokes of what happened to your husband. We need to know everything you can tell us." His eyes dropped to her empty hands. "Do you need something to drink? To eat?"

"I'm fine," she said.

"Then tell us about your husband."

CHAPTER
FOUR

OUR CLIENT TOOK a deep breath and squared her shoulders. "Harold and I met when he hit on me," she said, without embarrassment or preamble. "I was working an event, circulating with appetizers, and he waved me over. He had a wonderful deep voice and a courtly manner. I found him very easy to talk with. Almost effortless. He said, 'Young lady, I am not going to beat around the bush. I am struck by your beauty and spirit. I am attracted to you. I am older than you are, much older, but I am not going to let myself care about that. I've learned that life is too short to allow doubt to defeat the pursuit of meaning.'"

She'd told this story before, I could tell. It rolled off her tongue effortlessly. She'd probably been asked about their first meeting a million times.

"He asked for my number," she said. "I get asked for my number a lot. I know how to say no."

"Why did you say yes?" Danny said.

"Partly because I knew who he was," she said, again without hesitation. "But there was more to it than that. Harold was different. He was always a gentleman, but he was also direct and clear about what he wanted. He didn't play games. He had an energy, a fearlessness, that I responded to. I still have trouble expressing why I said yes."

"The two of you had chemistry."

Her eyes lit up. "We had *fun*, Mr. Hannity. He was so insightful and quick and caring and thoughtful. He told stories better than anyone. He knew everyone, and everyone knew him. We went places, met people, did things — interesting, important, fascinating things. I felt more alive with him than I've felt with anyone else. The more I got to know him, the angrier I became that we didn't meet sooner so that we could have more time together. I wished I'd been born decades earlier. It seemed unfair, like the universe had robbed us."

She stopped abruptly as she swallowed an upsurge of emotion.

Danny said, "Tell us about his charitable foundation."

She took a deep breath. "Harold loved San

Francisco, but he was also very critical of its short-comings, especially its failure with homelessness. His foundation supports food kitchens, shelters, drug clinics, mental-health treatment, and supportive housing in the city."

"I understand you are now in charge of the foundation."

"It's an issue I feel strongly about. As strongly as he did."

"The foundation is where most of his wealth now resides, correct?"

She nodded. "He left money to his daughter, son, and me — more than enough for us to live comfortably. The rest went to the foundation."

"How much?"

"How much?" she repeated, though she'd heard perfectly well. She folded her arms. Ah, money. The last taboo. The only topic in this liberated day and age that people still shy away from.

"The breakdown, please."

She frowned. "He left me ten million, the penthouse on Nob Hill, and the Napa estate. His daughter and son each got twenty million. The rest, about two hundred million, went to his foundation."

Yowza. I looked over at Barry and saw we were thinking the same thing: That added up to a quarter-billion reasons to want Harold Hawthorne dead.

"No other bequests?"

"A number of smaller bequests to old friends and long-time staff, totaling about two million."

"You're not comfortable with this discussion."

"No," she said, "I'm not. The money still isn't real to me. A year ago I was sharing a crappy apartment in the Outer Sunset with three roommates."

"Tell us about the night he died."

She went still. "We had dinner at home, in the penthouse."

"Who was there?"

"Harold and me, his son Holden, his daughter Julie, and a lawyer who's done work for him, Paul Barnard."

"No staff?"

She shook her head. "We have a cleaning service and we hire staff for events, but it's just the two of us at the penthouse."

"Tell us about his children and the lawyer."

"His son Holden is thirty-three, single, athletic. He traveled the world in his twenties — skiing and surfing, that kind of thing — but came back a few years ago to go to business school. Now he invests in startups."

"What kind of startups?"

"I'm not sure."

"Did he and Harold get along?"

"Yes and no. Harold wanted Holden to live life to the fullest — that was important to Harold — but he also wanted Holden to do something worthwhile."

"Is that why Holden went to business school and began investing?"

"Probably."

"Did Harold ever deny Holden anything?"

"Yes," she said. "Holden wanted his father to invest with him in certain startups. Harold wasn't convinced."

"Does Holden have his own money?"

"Enough for living expenses, travel, small investments, that kind of thing, but not enough for anything big."

"Did they argue?"

"Yes, but it's not like they had a huge fight or anything."

"So Holden was frustrated."

"Frustrated sounds right."

"Do you like him?"

"Do I like him?" she repeated. After a pause, she said, "I don't dislike him, if that's what you're asking."

"But he's not his father."

She shook her head. "Not in the slightest." Tears threatened again. Before things got too far, I handed her a tissue — I always keep them handy — and jumped in.

"I want to know about his daughter," I said. "You said her name is Julie?"

She took the tissue and wiped her eyes, grateful for the change of topic. "Julie's thirty-one, a year older than me. Single, attractive. She works for the Opera, does fund-raising and events."

"She doesn't need to work but has a job anyway?"

"She works because she's lonely," she said, then stopped, as if surprised. "I'm not sure why I said that. I'm not sure I've had that thought before."

Danny stepped in. "Her job keeps her busy and involved and working with other people. A reasonable way to spend one's time if one's goals include social engagement."

I resisted the urge to roll my eyes. Typical Boy Wonder nonsense — acknowledging the value of human interaction while simultaneously distancing himself from it. No doubt he was aware of the irony of him talking up the value of about being around people, and no doubt he was aware of my own assessment of his hermetic ways, but he kept his eyes on Claire. "Did Julie love her father?"

Claire nodded. "Very much. She's very much her daddy's girl."

"Which means she doesn't like you."

"Not at all."

"Is she the source of the rumors about you?"

"Which rumor are you referring to? " she said, holding Danny's gaze. "The one that accuses me of poisoning my husband?"

"We'll get to that. Did Julie have any reason to want her father dead?"

Claire shook her head. "I don't think so. Like I said, she loved her father."

"Was she upset about her inheritance?"

She shrugged. "I doubt it. She's not her brother. She's never felt a need to prove herself, at least not in a way that requires money. What she really wants is marriage and family."

"Was she upset about your father's foundation?"

"She felt slighted. She felt her father was favoring me over her."

"As indeed he was, Mrs. Hawthorne."

Her eyes narrowed. "Harold knew I care more about the foundation and its work than Julie does, and he knew I would be a better steward of his legacy."

I jumped in. "So basically, Julie needs to get over it?"

Claire turned toward me again. "Basically, yes."

"If she ever wanted to get involved in the foundation, would you let her?"

"Of course," she said right away, but I saw the idea hadn't occurred to her before. "If she wanted to."

Across from me, Barry cleared his throat. "Mrs. Hawthorne, tell us about Paul Barnard."

Startled, Claire blinked. The big galoot had been so still and quiet that she'd forgotten he was there. His ability to go into stealth mode and become invisible is a superpower, a claim I make without exaggeration because, let's face it, he's huge. Back in his bounty-hunter days, he'd show up at a perp's favorite hangout and turn into scenery and the regulars would forget he was there and let something slip and — *boom* — he'd know where to find his guy. No matter how many times I try the same trick, I always fail. I'm too jumpy. I'll still be twitching when they lay me in my grave.

"Paul did legal work for Harold," Claire said. "He's also a friend of Holden's — the two of them are the same age and know a lot of the same people."

"Does he know Julie?"

"Yes. I'm not sure how well."

Danny stepped back in. "What is he like as a person?"

She considered. "Smart. Personable. He's what I call a connector — good at introductions and networking."

"You don't like him."

She frowned. "I didn't say that."

"Are you disagreeing with me?"

"I'm — I don't know why you think that. I haven't said that."

Danny let it pass. "Is he involved in the foundation?"

"No, Harold had other lawyers for that."

"What about Harold's will? Was Mr. Barnard involved in drawing it up?"

She shook her head. "No, that was someone else as well."

"Did Mr. Barnard inherit anything from your husband? Will he get any business from the estate or the foundation as a result of your husband's death?"

"No and no."

Danny stretched his neck and shifted in his chair. "You understand why we're asking these questions, Mrs. Hawthorne. The police are investigating your husband's death as a homicide. If they're correct, then someone at your dinner table killed him. Everyone at that table had opportunity. Aside from you, at least two of them, Holden and Julie, had motive."

She started to protest, but Danny held up his hand.

"What I said is factual, whether you choose to acknowledge it or not. If you are innocent, then one or more of the others is guilty of murder."

Her lips tightened. For the first time, I saw a hint of fear in her beautiful blue eyes.

"Now," Danny said, "we need you to tell us about the dinner itself. We need to know everything there is to know about the night your husband was poisoned."

OUR CLIENT SAT SILENTLY for a moment, looking at each of us in turn, then nodded. "Ask away."

"What we know is limited to what we've read in the press," Danny said. "We know that you and your husband invited three guests to your Nob Hill apartment for dinner: Holden, Julie, and Paul. We know that three people at that table — Harold, Holden, and Paul — fell ill after consuming mushroom soup. We know the soup included a mushroom species that can be lethal when ingested. We know that Harold, Holden, and Paul were hospitalized. We know that Holden and Paul recovered, but that Harold died. Are these facts correct?"

"Yes," she said.

"Did you or Julie have any of the soup?"

"No."

"Why not?"

"Neither of us likes it. It's a family favorite, at least for Holden and Harold. I learned how to make it for them."

"You've made it before?"

"Dinner the first Sunday of the month is a family tradition. I make the soup for that."

"Where did you get the mushrooms?"

"From the garden. We have a small greenhouse on the rooftop deck."

"You picked the mushrooms yourself?"

"Yes."

"What steps are involved in the preparation of the soup?"

She considered. "It's an old family recipe, not at all complicated. I slice the mushrooms, sauté them in garlic and butter, then add them and few other ingredients to cream and chicken stock."

"Are you familiar with mushrooms?"

"Enough to know the difference between good mushrooms and lethal mushrooms,.."

"Are you sure of that?" Danny said. "The mushroom in question — *Amanita ocreata* — can be very difficult to distinguish from non-lethal species."

"When the doctors told us that Harold and Holden and Paul had mushroom poisoning, I immediately assumed the lethal mushroom came from the roof. I assumed I had missed it. I assumed" — her voice wavered — "that I was at fault."

"What changed your mind?"

"The police took away the mushroom garden and analyzed it and found no evidence of *A. ocreata*."

"You know this because?"

"Their questions changed. They started asking me about my travel and shopping. They asked to look at my Internet activity. They asked how much I knew about *A. ocreata*."

Which made sense. The lack of poisoned mushrooms on the roof was a puzzler. On the one hand, maybe it meant the mushrooms were added to the soup by someone other than Claire. On the other hand, maybe it meant Claire procured lethal mushrooms elsewhere so she could use a poison-free garden as part of her alibi. From the way things looked, the cops were leaning toward the latter theory.

"When the police asked you about your travel and shopping, what did you tell them?"

"Everything I could. I gave them full access — Internet, credit card purchases, bank account, the works."

"Has anything you've done or purchased, or any place you've been, provided you with access to lethal mushrooms?"

She nodded. "Harold and I often spent weekends at the Napa house. *A. ocreata* are found in forested areas throughout northern California."

So, to summarize: Our client was looking pretty thoroughly cooked. Motive: check. Opportunity: check. Means: check. It was a miracle the cops were letting her walk around free. Their willingness to do so meant they were probably tailing her. Which probably meant —

Danny interrupted my train of thought. "We'll need to speak with Julie and Holden, and with Paul Barnard. Can you bring them here?"

She blinked. "I doubt it. Julie doesn't like me. I get along well enough with Holden and Paul, but I'm pretty sure that all of them think I'm responsible for Harold's death."

Danny's mouth tightened. He knew what that meant: He'd have to go to them. Most definitely not his preferred scenario, given that it involved person-to-person social interaction in places that weren't his house or the bar.

"Where are the three of them likely to be?"

"When?"

"Right now and this evening."

"Paul has an office downtown. Holden is a workout fanatic and goes to the gym every day, often in the late afternoon. If the Opera has an event tonight, Julie might be there. I heard she's starting to get out and about. Let me check the Opera calendar." She pulled out her phone and hit an app and scrolled. "Tonight. An outreach event at City Hall."

"Do you have a lawyer who specializes in criminal defense, Mrs. Hawthorne?"

She shook her head.

"Then you need one. Immediately." He took a business card from his shirt pocket and handed it to her. "Luther Jackson. Tell him I sent you. He's an excellent defense attorney and can prepare you for what's likely to come."

"By likely to come you mean...."

"Your arrest for murder. The circumstantial evidence against you is strong. I expect the police and district attorney are readying charges as we speak."

Her face went pale. She had to know or suspect that, of course, but having it stated so plainly had to be disconcerting.

Danny stood up. "Mr. Rawlins and Mr. Sears and I have work to do. So do you."

She followed his lead and rose. "Thank you."

She picked up her handbag and turned to go, but then swung back. "Wait. We haven't talked about your fee."

"I charge one dollar for my services, plus expenses. Expenses include Mr. Rawlins and Mr. Sears at two hundred dollars an hour each."

She stared at him, puzzled. "One dollar?"

"I don't need the money. But I need skin in the game."

"If you say so," she said, but it was clear she didn't get it. Or rather, it was clear she didn't get *him*. She stood there and waited for him to say more, then realized he wasn't planning to utter another word. "I better go hire myself a lawyer."

"We'll be in touch, Mrs. Hawthorne."

With nod, she turned and left.

CHAPTER
SIX

AFTER WATCHING the lovely Claire walk away, Danny went into concrete-block mode. A few seconds passed, followed by a few more. Then he snapped out of it and said, "Do we all agree she's innocent?"

"As pure as the driven snow," I said.

"She loved him," Barry said.

Danny grunted with annoyance. "Then we don't have much time. Barry, the digital angle. Everything there is to know about everyone at that dinner table."

Barry nodded. Invisibility wasn't the big galoot's only superpower. He also knew how to find out stuff. I don't mean he was a computer ace or anything like that. He just knew who to ask — a consequence of years of finding people and, in a few cases, deliberately not finding them, if you get my meaning. If information was in a database somewhere, chances were good he knew someone with access to that database, and chances were good that person owed him.

Danny turned to me. "Is this room free tomorrow evening?"

"Let's find out."

We stepped into the bar's main room and plunked down on our stools. Jimmy finished serving a couple of slumming hipsters up front, then headed our way.

When Jimmy reached us, Danny said, "Dad, can we use the back room tomorrow night?"

Jimmy nodded. "That fast?"

"Looks like."

I frowned. What had I missed? Jimmy set three shot glasses on the bar and started pouring. I glanced at Barry, who looked at me and shrugged.

I cleared my throat. "Kid, you seem awfully confident."

"No reason not to be," he said as he watched the amber goodness fill his glass. "The only real challenge is the timing."

"You mean, for our client."

"More broadly." He was about to explain when I noticed his attention shift to the front. I turned and saw a familiar figure, her short trim frame a match for her short trim dark hair.

I sighed. The only problem with using Jimmy's as an office is that anybody can waltz in, including, in this case, the SFPD's very own Inspector Marissa Figueroa. A year behind Danny in the academy, the inspector was a good cop — smart and dogged and ambitious — but she was also insecure, a trait that sometimes caused us trouble. See, after Danny retired, the brass decided to push Inspector Figueroa as the department's new fresh face, and the good inspector had let that dubious honor get under her skin. She'd worked her butt off to get to where she'd gotten and hated the idea of anyone thinking of her as a token female or a token Latina or a token lesbian or a token anything. So she over-compensated every now and then. Acted too tough. Especially around Danny.

With a determined gait, she strode up to our barstools.

"Gentlemen," she said.

"Inspector," I said, "what can we do you for?"

"You know why I'm here."

"Do we?" I said, the essence of innocence.

Sometimes, the inspector played along. Some-times, she seemed to almost like us. But not today. Maybe she'd had a long week. Maybe the burden of the biggest case of her career was getting to her. "Why was Claire Hawthorne here?"

So my suspicion was right — the cops were tailing her.

I glanced toward Danny and Figueroa's eyes followed.

Danny looked up from his whiskey.

"Hello, Marissa."

"Danny."

"Mrs. Hawthorne is now my client."

She frowned. "Your client."

"You seem surprised."

"Just wondering if your famous gut got it wrong."

"You're here because you're about to arrest her. You want to arrest her, you're under pressure to arrest her, but there's that tiny sliver of doubt. You're worried about the egg on your face if you blow it."

She didn't answer, but the flash in her eyes betrayed her.

"Spill, Danny. What do you got?"

"Nothing you don't."

"If you're holding back —"

"You know I wouldn't do that. You have access to every fact I have and more — far more."

"And yet she's your client."

Danny shrugged. "This isn't a competition. We're after the same thing."

"We'll see about that."

He shrugged. "I'd caution against moving too fast — could be bad for your image."

She stiffened. "That how you're playing it?"

"Not me — you. Someday you'll realize that media attention matters for only one thing: gaining access to people you need access to."

"If you're holding back —"

"I can't withhold facts I don't know. Deduction isn't knowledge. Assertion without evidence is slander."

"You took her on without knowing all the facts."

He shrugged again. "Tell me I'm wrong. Show me I'm wrong. I'll drop Mrs. Hawthorne and help you make your case."

It had to be tempting to share what she had. She knew his track record, knew his methods, knew he didn't care who he embarrassed or angered. She knew he wouldn't hesitate to make a monkey out of her and the department if it suited his purposes.

But at the same time, in a universe of infinite possibilities, maybe he was wrong and she was right. How sweet that would be, beating the former Boy Wonder at his own game. How rewarding to outwit him and turn the tables on him and show him and the brass and the press and the whole damn city that Marissa Figueroa, the second-youngest homicide inspector in SFPD history, deserved her promotion and success.

Her eyes narrowed as she weighed her odds.

"I have a plan," Danny said. "A trap, if you will. But it will require your active participation."

"Go on," she said.

"Do you enjoy lying to murderers, Inspector Figueroa?"

She gave him a tight smile. "Do angels sing?"

"Then this is how it goes down."

He told us then, me and Barry and Jimmy and the good inspector. Described the trap, how the pieces fit together, and what our roles would be. It sounded crazy, but the instant he laid it out, my gut sensed he'd nailed it.

"Wait," I said, annoyed with him for, as usual, knowing exactly how to proceed. "How can you be so sure?"

"The circumstances point clearly in one direction," he said, then downed his shot in a single swift movement. "Our challenge isn't lack of certainty, which can and will be established, at least to our satisfaction, without difficulty. Our challenge is the lack of evidence to support an arrest, prosecution and conviction." He glanced at the inspector to gauge her willingness or ability to correct him, and when she didn't, he went on. "Even with the additional facts we gather, it's unlikely we'll have definitive proof or the means to gather it. It's essential that we plan carefully. Everything will need to line up for us to succeed."

The inspector stood there a moment, a scowl on her face, as she decided whether to play. Then she whipped out her phone and hit a button and, after a pause, said, "It's me. Hold off for now. We're working a new angle. No, not yet. I'll let him know. Yes. I'll deal with it."

She put the phone back in her pants. "You-know-who's not gonna be happy," she said, referring to the publicity-happy district attorney.

Danny shrugged. Like he cared.

The inspector looked at me and Barry. "You two on board with this?"

"Ready and willing," I said.

"Need anything from me?"

"Good to go."

She turned to Barry. "You know I can't help you. At all. In fact, if I learn anything about how you...."

"Understood," Barry said.

She turned to Danny. "What about you?"

Danny eased off his barstool and settled down on his bad leg. "Jake, how long will you need?"

I considered. "Three hours, tops."

He grabbed his cane. "Then why don't you join me."

"For what?" I jumped off my stool and shrugged on my coat.

"Three visits: a law office, a gym, and a party."

CHAPTER
SEVEN

MINUTES LATER, after reviewing the program, Danny and I were in the back of a cab, heading downtown. One thing I had to give the kid: Once he actually committed to detaching his lazy you-know-what from his overused couch, he didn't waste time. He built up speed fast, like a boulder hurtling down a cliff, and had no hesitation about dragging me and Barry along with him.

I suppose I could have chosen to be bothered by him acting like the boss of us. Anyone else pulling that stunt would get an earful of Jake. But with Danny it was different. When the kid was out there, throwing himself into other people's bad luck and figuring out how to make the world just a little bit better, I figured he'd earned his place as leader of the pack.

And truth was, I liked being part of it. Sure, chasing down leads interfered with my enjoyment of my favorite barstool while sipping Jimmy's whiskey and complaining vigorously about the state of the world, but fresh scenery every now and then made for a nice change of pace. And while I may be as worn as the sands of time, I'm still capable of feeling a nice buzz when I help a bad guy get his.

Or hers, as the case may be.

In the cab next to me, Danny's eyes were shut tight, his mouth compressed into a thin tense line, his hand gripping the strap of the seat belt he'd wrapped himself in. He hadn't been behind the wheel of a car since his crash and wasn't a fan of the other seats in a car, either. Had we not been a hurry, I knew he would have picked the train to get downtown.

Speaking of, something was bugging me. I cleared my throat. "I'm still not convinced you got this one," I said, which wasn't true but seemed as good an opening as any to pry loose exactly what he was up to. "How can you know for sure? And why are we moving so fast? There's still too much we don't know."

The eyes stayed shut, but the mouth did not. "Maybe I'm wrong."

Three simple words that, on the surface, seemed innocent and innocuous and inoffensive, but I knew better. My hackles shot up. And since you're probably wondering why my hackles are so touchy, I should explain that Danny-boy is the king of deflection. To the untrained ear, "maybe I'm wrong" comes across as a humble admission of fallibility — an acknowledgment by the great detective that he's as capable of error as the rest of us. But the reality is, the kid's been using that phony phrase since he was, well, a kid. He trots it out to divert, to push away, to avoid the bother of explaining, to shut down discussions he isn't in the mood to discuss. He uses those three words because once upon a time his mama told him that expressing doubt made him look more human and ordinary and relatable and less like a smug high-handed aloof non-explaining know-it-all.

"Someday," I said, "your impatience with reality is gonna lead you to really screw the pooch. I'd hate for that day to be today, when the lovely Claire is counting on us. I'd hate to have to apologize to her through a plate glass window at Chowchilla. If that happens, I'm gonna make you come with me so you can sit down in front of her and say, 'Sorry, Mrs. Hawthorne, I jumped the gun. I took the barest thread of supposition and wove a fantastical tapestry out of it, a tapestry made of nothing but guesswork and spit. Then I tried to sell the tapestry to the cops, but they didn't buy it because the damn thing fell to pieces as soon I held it up to the light. I did all that because I was in a hurry. I decided I'd try to solve the case and catch the killer in just two days. Probably because I wanted to get back to my stupid video game.'"

"Impatience with reality," Danny said, ignoring the heart of my complaint and focusing instead on a tiny irrelevant turn of phrase. He cocked his head and repeated the words, like he was savoring them. "Yes, that's apt."

"You bet your life it is," I shot back. "And don't you dare try to that deflection trick on me."

He gave me a sharp look but was saved from replying when the cab pulled to a stop. I looked out the window. We'd arrived in front of an office building in the heart of the financial district. People rushed past, eager to show us how important and busy they were. We climbed out of the cab. Danny settled his leg down, then aimed himself at the building entrance, flowing through the crowd like a cargo freighter in a packed harbor.

I glanced at the building directory next to the elevators and identified our destination: Paul Barnard, Attorney at Law. We'd called before we left the bar to make sure he was in his office and available to see us, which he was. According to the Internet, he was thirty-four years old and had opened his practice after graduating from Stanford Law. Striking out on one's own is a gutsy move for anyone, but for a lawyer — trained to prop up the status quo — that kind of gumption was notable. Paul's practice provided early-stage startups with the legal help they needed to move past the "all-nighters-in-the-garage" stage — incorporation, negotiating deals, and so forth.

The elevator door opened and we stepped in. Seconds later, the doors opened onto the eighth floor. A quick walk down a hallway brought us to Paul's office. With a turn of the knob, Danny pushed the door open into a space that looked more like an improvised startup than a traditional law office. It was a nice-size room — big windows, no walls, and a mish-mash of furniture. A long conference table and chairs anchored the back, next to the windows. A small kitchenette lined the wall on one side.

In the middle of the room, seated behind a desk stacked with law books, a young fellow dressed in Silicon Valley work gear — tan cargo pants and a blue button-down shirt — was looking at us from behind his laptop. He rose and made his way toward us. "Paul Barnard," he said, hand outstretched to Danny. "You must be Daniel Hannity. It's a pleasure to meet you. Your reputation precedes you."

Danny took the proffered hand, then gestured toward me. "My associate, Jake Sears."

Paul aimed his hand at me. "A pleasure." His grip was firm but not too firm, his smile easy and unforced, his eyes holding mine for just the right number of milliseconds. Like Claire said, this guy had the connector thing down pat. He was average height and build, with short brown hair and brown eyes. Not exactly handsome — his face was a bit too round for that — but he certainly seemed friendly enough.

He gestured toward the conference table. "Please, have a seat."

Danny and I sat across from each other while Paul took the chair at the end. I ran my eyes over the furniture, which seemed a bit on the hand-me-down side. The grey metal desk didn't match the beat-up mahogany conference table, which didn't match the modern black office chairs we were sitting in. Still, the place looked clean and neat and organized and there didn't seem to be anything in the room that didn't have a purpose. On the wall across the room, I spied a dark suit, white shirt, and thin black tie hanging from a hook, suggesting that Paul's evening activities required a different dress code.

Our host looked at me and then Danny. "I was surprised to get your call," he said, "but also relieved, in a way."

"Why is that, Mr. Barnard?" Danny said.

"I'm concerned about Claire. I've always liked her. I'm glad she's doing something to protect herself. I have a hard time accepting that she might have done it."

"By 'it,' you mean...."

"I find it hard to believe she intentionally poisoned Harold, Holden, and me."

"You've recovered from your bout, it seems."

He nodded. "It was awful. Beyond awful. I feel fortunate to be alive." He sat up straighter. "But enough about that. That's not why you're here. How can I help you?"

"We'd like your insight. Our working theory is that the police are mistaken in their determination that the Hawthorne's rooftop garden contained no lethal mushrooms."

"A reasonable line of defense."

"Do you have experience with criminal cases?"

"Not really. My focus is corporation law — con- siderably less interesting than crime. But I've provided support pro bono on several criminal cases."

"In terms of possible criminal charges relating to Mr. Hawthorne's death, I expect you've given this matter some thought."

"I have," he said. "I was there. I was poisoned. I nearly died. I know — knew — everyone at that dinner table. I'm very much an interested party."

"Did the police question you about the rooftop garden?"

"They asked about the garden, but I wasn't able to tell them much."

"Had you had the mushroom soup before? If so, did you have issues with it?"

"Once before, at a family dinner a few months ago. Everything that time was fine."

"On the fatal night, did you notice anything different about how the soup tasted or looked?"

"Sorry, no."

"Did Holden or Harold notice anything? I understand the soup was a favorite of theirs."

"I don't recall them saying anything."

"How about Julie? Did she say anything about the soup?"

His brow furrowed. "Not that I recall. But she wouldn't have. She didn't have any."

"I understand she doesn't like it."

"That's right." He gave us a look then, like he'd noticed an odd smell. "Why the question about Julie?"

"Just covering our bases, Mr. Barnard."

He stared at Danny for a long second. "I don't buy that. After you called, I read up on you. A crash course, if you will."

Danny stayed silent, waiting for Paul to continue.

"I learned something about your reputation and your style. I learned you get results. Which indicates that your questions — all of them — have intent. So let me be clear: I'm glad to help you help Claire. I'll do all I can, legally and ethically, in that regard. But I'm not interested in helping you transfer suspicion or jeopardy to Julie."

"The two of you are close?"

"We're friends."

"As you are with Holden."

"Yes." He looked like he wanted to say more, but instead changed tack. "I have to ask: What is this? A fishing expedition?"

"Not at all," Danny said. "Our theory is well-developed."

"And supported by new evidence, from the sound of it."

"There is one other topic I'd like to broach. I

don't mention this lightly, and I mean no offense in asking it."

Paul's eyebrows rose. "Please, go ahead."

Danny reached into his jacket pocket and pulled out a clear plastic bag. Inside was a sheet of white paper. He laid the sheet on the table and pushed it toward Paul, who leaned forward and read the words on the sheet, handwritten in block letters: "MURDERER!   YOU   DESERVE   WHAT'S COMING."

Paul leaned back. "Wow."

"This was slipped under Claire Hawthorne's penthouse door this morning, sometime after seven and before ten. We established the timeframe after interviewing Claire and her building's doorman. I'm afraid I have to ask: Where were you this morning?"

Paul took a deep breath, then exhaled. "No offense taken. At seven, I was at the gym, getting in an early workout. I came straight here — the gym's a couple of blocks away — for a client meeting at nine. Aside from a quick run downstairs for a sand-wich at lunch, I've been here all day."

"I assume you can, if needed, provide corrob-oration?"

"Yes."

Hook planted, it was my turn.

"This place," I said, gesturing to the room, "doesn't look like any law office I know."

Paul gave me an apologetic shrug. "It seems to work for my clients."

"Startups, mostly, right?"

He nodded. "There's a B2B incubator two floors up that provides space to several dozen startups. I set up shop here to be close to them. The startup founders are usually young and prefer casual, so when it came to furnishing this space, I didn't sweat it."

"Your practice is just you?"

"Yes. Which has proved a mistake. I started three years ago with me and my laptop. I'm used to working solo. I've had trouble accepting that I need help."

I spied a gym bag on the floor next to his desk and pointed to it. "Is that how you met Holden?"

His eyes followed. "We go to the same gym."

"I hear he's a fitness freak."

"Totally. Puts me to shame."

"How's he taking his dad's death?"

"Hard. As you'd expect."

"Did he and his father get along?"

Paul frowned. "Gentlemen, I'll repeat: I have no interest in a fishing expedition."

"Hey," I said, "I'm just asking a question."

"No, you're not." He stood up. "I'm afraid I can't give you any more time."

We clambered to our feet. Danny said, "Thank you for meeting with us, Mr. Barnard."

"Listen," Paul said, a note of apology in his voice, aware he'd been abrupt. "I want to help Claire. If I can do that in a way that doesn't cast suspicion or interest on Julie or Holden, let me know."

"Thank you," Danny said. "We'll be in touch."

We waited until we were outside the building to talk.

"Well?" I said.

He glanced at his watch. "Did Barry text?"

I pulled out my phone and saw that he had. "We're good."

"Then let's go."

THE GYM where Paul and Holden worked out was a couple blocks away, in a building that once upon a time housed an actual stock exchange. A big tall row of Roman columns, built to impress, rose like guardians up front. The building's transformation into a high-end exercise space had to be a bit deflating for those who, back in the day, engaged in the pulse-pounding frenzy of the trading floor. These days, the only heart-pumping and breath-puffing came from bench presses and exercise classes.

At the front desk, a fit young fellow handed us two guest passes. "Your guy's doing weights," he said. "Give Mr. Rawlins my regards." I wondered briefly how the young fellow had crossed paths with Barry, and what Barry had done for him. The breadth and reach of the big guy's network never ceased to surprise.

We made our way into a big open room filled with exercise machines whose purposes were, frankly, baffling. I'm a fan, at least from a theoretical standpoint, of pushups and situps and the like. But these machines, with their pulleys and cables and strangely positioned bars and oddly inclined benches, looked like they belonged in a high-tech torture chamber, an association reinforced by the wheezes and gasps of their willing victims.

The Internet had shown us pictures of Holden, so picking him out at the far end of the torture chamber was a snap. He was a good-looking guy, tall and fit, with surfer-dude blond hair, dressed in high-end workout gear. As we approached, he was holding a big barbell loaded with weights on his shoulders and, with focus and effort, was doing squats like nobody's business. I had to admit I was impressed. He was putting in the kind of exercise that Danny needed to do more of, with a level of enthusiasm that Danny could only dream of.

We waited for him to finish his set, then stepped closer. He was breathing hard, his hair wet with sweat. When he realized we were looking at him, he frowned, clearly wondering why the blond giant with the cane and the skinny guy with the mad-inventor hair were staring at him.

"Mr. Hawthorne," Danny said. "We're here at the request of Claire Hawthorne."

Holden's frown deepened. "Do I know you?"

"My name is Daniel Hannity. I'm a private detective." He nodded toward me. "My associate, Jake Sears."

"Private detective?"

"Mrs. Hawthorne hired us."

He blinked in surprise. "Claire hired you? For what?"

"To prove her innocence."

He seemed taken aback.

"You think she's guilty," Danny said.

Holden's mouth opened and stayed open for a few seconds before any words came out. "It's not that I think she did it on purpose...."

"You think it was an accident."

"She made the soup. She grew the mushrooms."

"If she were found liable for your father's death, what would happen to your father's fortune?"

He flushed. "What do you mean?"

"Would she still be in control of it?"

"Of course not."

"You and Julie would assume control."

"According to our lawyers. Not that that's your concern."

"On the contrary, Mr. Hawthorne. It's of paramount concern."

"I don't think so. Not for you. We're done here." He picked up a towel, wiped sweat from his forehead, then reached down and grabbed a set of hand weights. His intent was clear — he wanted us to vamoose — but when he saw we weren't budging, he paused, a weight in each hand.

"I don't expect you to understand," he said, his eyes zeroing in on the extra pounds wrapped around Danny's middle, "but this workout is important. It's taken me weeks to recover enough to start pushing again."

"We just met with Mr. Barnard," Danny said. "He said the poisoning was 'beyond awful'."

"Yeah, that's right." Realizing we weren't going to go away without at least a little satisfaction, he returned the weights to their rack, then turned back toward us. "I can't help you. I don't know how the mushrooms ended up in the soup. I've told the police everything I know. You should talk to them."

"Do you care what happens to Claire?"

"That's a trick question. If she poisoned me and Dad and Paul on purpose, then I want her to fry. But if she didn't...."

"Then we won't take up any more of your time, Mr. Hawthorne. Thank you for speaking with us." Danny pivoted and headed toward the exit

Holden watch him go, a puzzled look on his face. I tossed him a farewell shrug, then followed Danny.

Outside the gym, I said, "A bit short there at the end. I thought the plan was to show him the bait."

"No need to." He glanced at his watch. "Last stop." Without another word, he aimed us toward the subway station.

CHAPTER
NINE

IT WOULD HAVE BEEN a lot easier and faster to hop in a cab, but when Danny decides we have time to avoid the comfort and convenience of a motor vehicle, the inevitable outcome is that no internal combustion engine is going to do our work for us. Instead, we walked ten minutes along streets congested with commuters, down a flight of stairs into the train station, through a pay turnstile, then down more stairs to the subway platform, where we crammed ourselves into a train that was already packed to the gills with people who wanted to be there about as much as I did.

Though Danny avoids individual people as a matter of general principle, he doesn't mind being lost in a crowd. He goes into a zone — not concrete-block mode, since he's able to move more than his eyelids — where he's aware of his environment but floating through it. Something dreamier, more contemplative.

Unlike my zone, which was best described as resentful and annoyed.

The train pulled into the station near City Hall. After walking through the station's urine-drenched corridors, we emerged into the last remaining shreds of daylight. Rising before us, across a vast open plaza, stood the impressive dome of San Francisco City Hall. I'm not a gusher as a rule — grousing and whining is more my groove — but I freely admit that our fair city's seat of power is about as grand it gets, at least on the Left Coast. It's a true beauty of a building, soaring above everything around it. The closer you get, the bigger you realize it is.

The real treat, in my humble view, is what's inside: marble everywhere, with a vast inner rotunda and a dramatic sweeping staircase that practically pulls your eyes upward. The space was being used that evening by the San Francisco Opera for one of the "demographic desperation" events they throw every now and then, when management takes a look at their audience and realizes that the median age is somewhere between doddering and dead. Instead of stuffy black-tie, the vibe was hip and casual. Our less-than-snazzy attire — sports jacket and t-shirt for me, bland button-down shirt and jeans for Danny — didn't raise an eyebrow.

A waiter wandered our way with a tray of tiny little sausages wrapped in a flaky dough. I signaled to him and grabbed three and wolfed them down.

Our quarry, according to the Internet, was slim and attractive, with shoulder-length brown hair. Danny used his height to scan the room. When he locked in, my eyes followed. At one side of the rotunda, standing behind an information table, Julie Hawthorne was handing a brochure to a pair of twentysomething hipsters whose only previous exposure to opera was "Kill the Wabbit" on YouTube. She was dressed in a simple black cock-tail dress that covered her shoulders, her hair pulled back in a ponytail. Even from across the room, I could tell she was tired. Her father had died less than a month ago. She wasn't working the event with a fake smile plastered on her face because she wanted to. She was here, I guessed, because grieving alone at home was worse. Nothing gets staler faster — or stinkier, I thought, glancing at Danny — than shutting yourself away and wallowing in what you've lost.

The hipsters drifted off and Julie sighed, her eyes wandering the room. She frowned when she saw us. Her lips compressed as she zeroed in on Danny's cane and my hair. Someone — Paul or Holden — had warned her.

"I know who you are," she said when we got to her table. "I have nothing to say to you."

I whipped out the piece of paper in the plastic bag with "MURDERER" scrawled on it and held it in front of her.

"Claire found this under her door this morning."

She snorted. "She probably wrote it herself."

"You think she killed your father," Danny said.

"Of course I do," she said, her voice, even amid the din, louder than it needed to be.

"Why are you so sure?"

She slammed Danny with a look I'd never want aimed at me — fury fueled by grief — and nearly followed it with a roar of rage before remembering where she was and pulling back from the brink, barely.

At that moment, Paul Barnard appeared, out of breath, like he'd been rushing to get here. He'd changed into the suit and tie we'd seen hanging in his office.

"Julie," he said.

Startled, her attention shifted to him. "Paul, what are you doing here?"

He moved to her side, his hand finding its way to the small of her back. "I heard from Holden, so I knew these two would be heading here next."

"You didn't have to," she said, shifting away. "There was no need. I'm fine."

"They're stirring up trouble."

Julie's gaze returned to us. "I want you to leave now. Your client's going to rot in hell for what she did."

"Ms. Hawthorne," Danny said. "Please accept my condolences for your loss. One thing I have learned is that anger offers only temporary relief from the grief of a loved one's passing. Time is the true healer. Time and, in your case, the knowledge that justice can prevail if you allow it."

"Get the hell out of here."

There was really nothing to say after that, so Danny and I complied.

Back outside, breathing in the cool evening air, I was about to ask Danny if he'd noticed what I noticed when he whipped out his phone and called

Barry and told him to be on the lookout for the very thing I'd noticed.

"You sure this is gonna work?" I said, looking up at his hulking form.

"She needs to be there," he muttered. "If she isn't...."

"No daughter, no dice?"

"No Julie, no justice."

CHAPTER
TEN

A LAWYER, a gym rat, and a society gal walk into a bar. I'm sure I've heard a joke that starts like that.

But the gathering at Jimmy's Bar, held the evening after our encounter with Julie, was no laughing matter. I'd spent the day getting my contributions just right. Barry's network of contacts had coughed up several interesting tidbits that, while in no way conclusive, helped cast light on the truth. Danny had pulled into Jimmy's after lunch and, from his command barstool, spent most of the afternoon in concrete-block mode, unthawing only to bark out more orders.

The invite, which had gone out that morning to Julie Hawthorne, Holden Hawthorne, and Paul Barnard, requested their presence at Jimmy's that evening at six. Daniel Hannity, private eye when he wanted to be, had uncovered important information about the death of Harold Hawthorne and wished to share it with them first.

The first indication that we'd stirred the hornet's nest had come an hour after the email went out, when the good inspector called to report that Julie had rung her, furious, and begged the inspector to tell Claire and her "blond neanderthal" private eye to you-know-what themselves. "I told her I couldn't do that," the inspector said, "but I told her I'd be there for support."

"Did she bite?"

"Not sure. But I like her style. 'Blond neanderthal' — that's pretty good."

"I'll pass along your regards."

Around half past five, Claire arrived with her new lawyer, Luther Jackson. In the courtroom, Jackson was a charm machine, but with Danny he didn't bother. He bulldozed straight up to him. "This is one crazy harebrained stunt."

Danny shrugged. "I'm here. You're here. What can go wrong?"

"You sure Figueroa's on board?" Like all good defense attorneys, distrust of officialdom was baked into his DNA.

"If you have a better idea, I'm all ears."

He stared hard at Danny for a few seconds, his shaved ebony head gleaming in the bar's dim light, then turned to his client. "We don't have to do this. There are other ways."

Claire shook her head. "We're here. I want to try."

I remembered again why I liked this gal. She had grit — in spades.

Ten minutes before the appointed hour, Inspector Figueroa strode in.

"Not yet," I said in answer to her unspoken question.

"In eleven minutes," she said with a glance at her watch, "if and when they don't show, we do it my way."

"Stop your worrying," I said. "They'll be here."

At two minutes to six, much to my relief, the bar door swung open and the aforementioned threesome walked in.

I jumped off my barstool to greet them. None was happy to see me. Julie was dressed in dark pants and cream sweater, with a blue scarf around her neck. Holden, no slouch in the style department, was freshly showered, with dark slacks and white-button-down shirt. Paul, in his Silicon Valley casual, looked like he'd come straight from his office.

"Thank you for coming," I said, then led them into the back room.

The crowd already there — Danny, Barry, Inspector Figueroa, Claire, and Jackson — swiveled toward us when we stepped in.

For a long second, everyone eyed everyone, unsure how to proceed.

"I appreciate your attendance this evening," Danny said to the threesome.

Jimmy poked his head in. "Who's having what?"

Holden and Julie and Paul exchanged glances. "Water," Holden said, and the others nodded in agreement.

"Please," Danny said, "have a seat."

Per Danny's instructions, the room had been arranged into a replica of the fatal dinner, with a table in the middle of the room with seating for five, and chairs for the rest of us along the walls.

Danny stepped to Harold Hawthorne's seat at the head of the table. As instructed, Claire stepped to her chair at the other end. Without being told what to do, Holden and Julie and Paul approached the seats they knew they were assigned: Holden and Paul on Danny's right, Julie opposite.

Jimmy appeared with five glasses of water, set them on the table, then left the room, shutting the door firmly behind him.

Danny sat down and adjusted his leg. "Please, have a seat. Let's get started." The trio looked at each other. After a second, Paul shrugged and took his seat, the others following.

"Thank you," Danny said. "You are all here as my guests at a private event at my invitation. You are under no legal obligation to be here. Your reasons for being here are your own. You may be here to see justice done, to protect someone from legal injury, out of simple curiosity, or some combination of the above."

He gestured to the rest of us. "I've invited several other guests. Mr. Jackson is Mrs. Hawthorne's attorney. Mr. Rawlins and Mr. Sears are my associates."

He pointed to the good inspector. "All of you have met Inspector Figueroa. She is here as an observer and a guest. She is not here in an official capacity. She will not be asking questions. She accepts that this is a private event, hosted by me. I stress this point to ensure no misunderstanding. Your participation in tonight's discussion is voluntary. You are here because you choose to be here."

"Are you going to get to the point?" Holden said. "We don't have all day."

"Yes, Mr. Hawthorne, I'm going to get to the point. Everyone in this room is aware that Harold

Hawthorne died after ingesting lethal mushrooms. The questions the police have been asking are: Were the mushrooms in the soup added accidentally or deliberately? If the latter, was the intent to murder? If so, who and why and how?"

No one spoke. That was the thing about Danny — he knew how to hold a room.

"To prove a case of murder, the police and district attorney must determine means, motive and opportunity." He gestured to his client. "Harold's wife Claire, for example, had an excellent motive. She'd recently gained control of his fortune. Perhaps, to ensure he didn't change his mind about that, she killed him."

Claire's lips tightened, but she kept them shut.

Danny's attention turned to Julie. "Or you and your brother. If the media reports are to believed, you were hurt and angered when your father chose Claire to run his foundation. Perhaps you did something about it. Perhaps you killed your father and attempted to frame his widow."

Julie's nostrils flared. "I can't believe we have to put up with this —"

"You're free to leave, Ms. Hawthorne," Danny said. "If you don't want to be here, go."

"But I —"

"You're here by invitation. I don't need you here.

If you don't want to find out who killed your father, go."

Julie's mouth opened and stayed open. Then she shut it. "I didn't say I wanted to go."

"Then you'll let me continue."

She was really hating Danny in that moment, but she'd boxed herself in. "It's your party," she said, crossing her arms and leaning back in her chair.

Danny's eyes remained on her for three long seconds. "You and your brother could have other, non-financial motives, of course. Maybe you killed your dad because he was a rotten father."

"He wasn't —" she said, then stopped. She glanced at her brother before continuing. "Daddy wasn't always attentive or supportive, but that's neither here nor there."

Danny's eyes swung toward her brother Holden. "You're keeping quiet."

"So?" Holden said.

"Anything to add?"

Holden smirked. "No."

Danny sighed. "I understand you've been meeting with various startups about coming aboard as an investor."

"And?"

"I understand you've identified several

promising opportunities and are eager to move forward."

Holden straightened his back. "And?"

"I'm told that with several of them, you promised your father's support in addition to yours."

"Now wait a minute —"

"Apparently because, on your own, you lack sufficient resources for a seat at the table."

That got his goat. He sat forward. "Who said that?"

"Not your concern."

"Like hell."

"It must have angered you when your father decided to put most of his fortune into a foundation instead of pass it on to you."

"I want to know who told you about the deals I'm working on."

"I'm not sharing my sources, Mr. Hawthorne."

"I don't have to put with this."

"Then go. You're free to leave. I don't need you here."

That flummoxed him. He sat back.

"Wait, I —"

"If you want to know who killed your father, you'll stay."

Holden sat there for a few long seconds,

stewing in his seat, conscious of all eyes on him and not liking it.

"Of course I was upset about the foundation and Claire," he finally said, his eyes flickering toward her briefly. "There's a lot at stake. Claire's a nice-enough person, but she's not experienced in business."

"Unlike you," Danny said, encouraging him.

"I'm an investor and adviser in multiple star-tups," he said.

"Meaning startups humor you and your ideas in exchange for much-needed cash."

It took him a second. "Humor?"

On cue, I stepped to the table and handed Danny a folder. He set the folder on the table in front of him and opened it. A simple act, really, but it felt like an unveiling — like vital secrets were about to be disclosed.

"I have a list of your investments. A hundred thousand here, a quarter of a million there. Pocket change. If any of these companies takes off, you'll make out like a bandit. But so far, not a single one of your supposedly savvy investments has paid off. You've invested close to two million dollars in eight startups and have nothing to show for your efforts."

"How did you get that information?"

Danny ignored the question and ran a finger along the last line on the sheet of paper. "Your ongoing discussions with 3D printing startup XerXes intrigue me. They're a confident bunch. Not many startups go into meetings with a firm demand for five million minimum from prospective investors."

Holden frowned. "The 3D printing field is —"

"Vastly overhyped," Danny said. "But not my point. My point is, you don't have five million. You needed your father's support. When you talked with him about the opportunity, what did he say?"

"How —" he said, then stopped himself. "What my father and I may or may not have talked about is none of your business."

"Except in this case. This obscure little startup, one of many wannabes in a field floating on gossamer dreams, is at the heart of all of this." He turned his gaze toward the legal eagle at the table. "Mr. Barnard, please help me here. This company, XerXes, first approached Holden about a year ago, correct?"

Paul arranged his lawyer face into a frown. "I don't see what that has to do with anything."

"Humor me, Mr. Barnard. Please. I ask your forbearance."

"Yes," Paul said cautiously. "The timeframe sounds right."

"I believe you helped make the introduction."

"Yes."

From my seat against the wall, I had a full unobstructed view of him. He seemed puzzled, like he wanted to be patient and helpful but doubted that Danny's line of questioning had any value.

"You know the company's founders," Danny said. "You helped them incorporate. You've been acting, unofficially, as their general counsel."

"That's not something I can discuss, Mr. Hannity. I fail to see the relevance."

"It's relevant because you undoubtedly were involved in their decision to approach Holden with a request for a minimum commitment of five mill."

"I can't discuss that. You know that."

"I also know that you and Holden are friends. The two of you met three years ago, I believe. Through him, you met Julie."

At the mention of her name, Julie shifted in her seat.

Holden shot a quick glance at his sister, then swung his eyes back to Danny. "You say that like it means something."

As for my eyes, I was keeping them firmly on Paul. I will say this: The guy was no dummy. He was many things, but dummy was not one of them. Even as his shoulders very subtly stiffened, the expression on his face remained puzzled. "Mr. Hannity," he said, "I'm not sure of the relevance, but yes, it's through Holden that I met Julie and Mr. Hawthorne and Claire, for that matter. That's how life happens. You meet someone, and they introduce you to someone else, and so on."

Danny kept his eyes on Paul. "You're a skillful communicator, Mr. Barnard. For example, just now, in three simple sentences, you masked and simultaneously reassured. You made your calculated ingratiation of the Hawthorne clan seem natural and organic — the happy result of circumstance rather than a plan."

Paul's eyebrows rose. "A plan?"

"Harold Hawthorne was impressed with you, wasn't he, Mr. Barnard. A self-starter with brains and charm. He saw ambition and intelligence, even daring, in you."

"Mr. Hannity, I —"

"If you don't mind, Mr. Barnard. Harold decided to give you a piece of business. It was a test and you both knew it. You passed, of course. So he kept giving you more. Gradually, he began to trust you."

"I'm trying my best to remain patient here."

"Good. Keeping doing that. Several months ago, something in your relationship with Harold changed. I don't know the exact cause of that change, though I do know the result: He stopped entrusting you with pieces of business. When Harold announced his charitable foundation two months ago, you were caught flat-footed. You had no idea. You realized your influence over the Hawthorne fortune was slipping away."

Paul's mouth opened. He looked surprised, even hurt. If I hadn't known better, I would have believed he was both. "Mr. Hannity," he said, with just the right amount of bewilderment, "what you're implying is outrageous."

"On that we agree," Danny said. "The murder of Harold Hawthorne and the framing of his wife are the stuff of nightmares — brutal in their calculation, breathtaking in their lack of remorse."

A spot of color appeared on the lawyer's cheeks. "I don't have to sit here and listen to insults."

"I can't stop you from walking out that door," Danny said. "Inspector Figueroa may feel differently."

From her chair behind him, the good inspector said, "Mr. Barnard, I would appreciate your cooperation in this matter."

The red in Paul's cheeks got deeper. He

swiveled around and looked her in the eye. "And if I don't choose to cooperate?"

"I would appreciate your cooperation."

He could have pressed the point and knew it, but instead he chose to back off. "Of course, Inspector." His gaze returned to Danny. "Mr. Hannity, I'd recommend you proceed carefully."

"Let's talk about mushrooms," Danny said. "Specifically, the species called *Amanita ocreata*, known commonly as the Angel of Death, found throughout Northern California, including in Salt Point State Park near the town of Jenner."

At the mention of the town's name, Julie's back stiffened.

Danny continued. "You spent time in Jenner recently, Mr. Barnard. A full weekend, in fact, one month before Harold Hawthorne was murdered."

Paul had to be on high alert now, but not a lick of worry made it through the mask of impatience on his face.

"Let's say that's so," he said.

"A romantic getaway for two, I believe."

Paul's nostrils flared, but aside from that — nothing. "I don't feel comfortable discussing that."

"Does Holden know?"

Holden sat up. "Do I know what?"

Paul shook his head. "Dude, the guy is cage-rattling. I'll explain later."

Julie stiffened. "You'll explain *what* later?"

"Julie," Paul said.

"Don't Julie me. You promised."

Holden said, "Promised? What did you promise?"

I had to bite my lip to keep from grinning. Am I a bad person that I really enjoy watching liars squirm?

Danny was more than ready to explain the nature of that promise, but Julie beat him to it. Looking her brother square in the eye, she said, "Paul and I were dating. Secretly."

"What?" Holden said.

"That's right," Paul said to Holden, a perfectly calibrated hint of relief in his voice, like he was eager to unload a burden. "Julie and I are dating."

"*Were* dating," Julie said.

"Wait," Paul said, swiveling toward her. "*Were*?"

"Most definitely past tense," she said with barely a glance at him, her focus on her brother. "Until I knew for sure how I felt, I didn't want Daddy to know."

Holden looked hurt. "You thought I'd blab?"

She gave her brother a look that would have

chilled Satan on a hot summer day. Clearly, his mouth had a history.

Unable to withstand her gaze, Holden transferred his confusion and hurt to Paul. "Dude," he said. "Not cool."

I nearly grinned again. Ah, the breaking of the Bro Code: Thou Shalt Not Bang Thy Bud's Sister.

"I wanted to tell you," Paul said, "but...." He shrugged and gestured toward Julie.

Danny stepped in. "Ms. Hawthorne, during your weekend in Sonoma, was there a period of time in which when you and Mr. Barnard were not together?"

"No," she said. "We drove up and back together. We stayed at a bed-and-breakfast. On Saturday we went for a hike. We were together the whole time...."

She trailed off. Paul's eyes shot toward her.

"Except for when?" Danny said, prompting her.

"We drank a lot Saturday night," she said. "And I ... zonked out. When I woke up the next morning, Paul wasn't there. He came back with muffins and coffee. He said he wanted to let me sleep in...." She looked at him then, like she was reinterpreting what had gone down that morning.

"Do you have anything to add, Mr. Barnard?"

Paul shook his head. "No."

"No explanation of where you were while Julie slept? No description of what you were doing?"

"Again, I fail to see the relevance. We're talking about muffins and coffee? Really?"

"Yes, Mr. Barnard, really. Did you leave Ms. Hawthorne to gather muffins and coffee? Or did muffins mask your real purpose?"

Paul sighed. "I'm beginning to tire of this."

"That's unfortunate, because we're just getting started. When you went for muffins, did you go anywhere else?"

Paul said nothing as he weighed how to respond.

Danny leaned forward and said, very softly, "That's right, Mr. Barnard. You'll want to consider your answer carefully. A lie now, so soon after being caught in a falsehood about your fling with Julie, would undermine your credibility even further."

In all fairness, Paulie-boy was in a tough spot. He had to be wondering if traffic cams had caught him doing something other than choosing between blueberry and banana-nut. He knew that Inspector Figueroa had the resources to find any footage that existed; if it did exist and she had it, then claiming he was a muffin-focused lothario that morning would be foolish and damaging. But if, on the other hand, there was no footage and he admitted going somewhere he didn't have to admit going, then it was likely he'd be kicking himself later.

He could have clammed up, of course. That would have been the prudent thing to do. He could have said nothing and stood up and walked out. But the Paul Barnards of this world — confident, ambitious, willing to take risks — aren't good at stepping back from a challenge. Caution isn't one of their strengths. He'd spent his life believing he was smarter than everyone else and wasn't about to stop believing that now. So I wasn't surprised when Paulie-boy rolled the dice and said:

"I have nothing to hide. I still fail to see the relevance, but I'm happy to tell you that I felt like a morning hike, so I went on one."

"Where did you go, Mr. Barnard?"

Another tough decision. Had he been caught on video? In for a penny....

"Along the trails in the park."

Danny nodded. "Thank you, Mr. Barnard."

Paul's eyes narrowed. "No thanks are required."

"On the contrary. Thank you for taking us back to our topic: lethal mushrooms. Salt Point State Park is known for *A. ocreata*. Visitors are warned to avoid them. Did you know that, Mr. Barnard?"

"I don't know. I don't remember."

Julie frowned. "We talked about the mushrooms. Joked about them."

"Sorry," he said to her. "I don't remember that."

"You remember everything," she said. "We've talked about that, too. Mind like a steel trap and so on. Or maybe you don't remember that either?"

Paul threw her a look but stayed quiet.

Danny cleared his throat. "Means, motive, and opportunity are crucial in an investigation. Harold Hawthorne was killed by lethal mushrooms. His killer needed access to these mushrooms. You, sir, had access."

Paul shook his head. "You haven't proved that."

"No, sir. You did, just now, when you admitted to everyone in this room that you were alone in Salt Point State Park that morning. Indisputably, you had access."

The spot of color returned to Paul's cheeks.

"Now," Danny said, "let's turn to opportunity. On this point, at least, I expect we can all agree that everyone at dinner that evening had opportunity."

"I don't agree with that," Paul said.

"Did you step into the kitchen at any point, Mr. Barnard?"

"I don't recall."

"Were you in the presence of the others at all times? Was there not even a single moment when you were alone before you sat down to dinner? You didn't use the bathroom, for example? You didn't wash your hands before dinner?"

"I don't recall."

For someone young and healthy and in apparent full possession of his faculties, Paulie-boy was forgetting an awful lot of stuff. And everyone sensed it. Any doubt that might have existed in the room was quickly vanishing. Every single set of shoulders was tense. Every single eye was riveted on Paulie-boy and Danny. Across the table from our target, Julie was biting her lip and trembling. Holden, seated next to Paulie-boy, was staring dumbfounded at his friend, mouth open like a stunned fish. At the end of the table, Claire's fists were busy clenching and unclenching like nobody's business.

"Did you offer to help Claire in the kitchen, while she was getting dinner prepared? Did you stir the mushroom soup as it simmered on the stove? Did you help transfer the soup to a serving bowl? Did you carry the soup to the dinner table?"

The answer to all of those questions was yes, of course.

"Meaningless questions," Paul said, with an impatient wave. "Even if I did, it proves nothing."

"On the contrary: It establishes opportunity. I

repeat: All of you — including you, Mr. Barnard — had opportunity to tamper with the soup."

"I don't accept your premise."

"Yes, you do. You're just not willing to admit it."

Anger slipped through Paul's mask then. Maybe that was the moment he realized that Danny was no ordinary opponent. Maybe that was when the fear began to creep in.

Danny barreled on. "The establishment of motive is the most difficult piece of this puzzle. Not the motive itself — control of the Hawthorne fortune is motive enough — but understanding how that motive applies to you. After all, you inherited nothing from Harold Hawthorne. Your legal practice gains no new business as a result of his death."

"Finally," Paulie-boy said, "something we agree on."

"We researched you, Mr. Barnard. You're an intelligent, capable, hardworking individual. You attended a top law school and graduated near the top of your class. You present well in social gatherings. One would think that someone with your skills would find himself with a plethora of opportunities.

"But you did not and do not, Mr. Barnard. The reason you started your own practice is because no one would hire you. You interned at two different law firms during law school, neither of which offered you a job when you graduated. You applied for positions at other firms, but none took you on. The reason for that is simple: Once people get to know you, they don't like you. They don't like you because you're a sociopath."

The spot of color on Paul's cheeks flamed, but he didn't respond.

"The energy you put into networking is an adaptive response to your lack of empathy. You're self-aware enough to realize you're missing a crucial aspect of what it means to be human, and intelligent enough to understand that this lack has held you back. To mask your sociopathy, you've carefully studied human emotional response and developed techniques to conform to human social conventions and expectations. Over time, you've built a mask that works well for superficial and introductory relationships. You know what people want to hear, you know what they expect, you know how to ingratiate yourself. It's only when people get to know you better that they see through the mask. It takes time for them to see the coldness inside."

"You've got this all wrong," Paulie-boy said.

"It's why, three years after graduating with

highly marketable skills in the midst of a tech-nology boom, you're still bottom-feeding your legal expertise, placing yourself two floors below a sea of young entrepreneurs, leveraging their inexperience and lack of time to generate enough income for you to continue on, just barely."

"Is this your game plan, Mr. Hannity?" Paul said. "Insult me to see what happens?"

Danny gestured toward Holden. "The younger Mr. Hawthorne, of course, has always been too self-involved to notice your flaws. He accepted your calculated social behaviors as expressions of true friendship. You understood his narcissism and will-ingly fed it. This so-called friendship served you both."

Holden stirred as he tried to catch up, but Danny plowed on. "Julie, on the other hand," he said, turning his attention to her, "was a tougher sell, wasn't she, Mr. Barnard? Unlike her brother, she's no preening narcissist. In fact, she's the oppo-site: an insecure pleaser. Which presented a problem for you. When you developed your plan to poison the mushroom soup, you recognized the possibility that Holden might die. If he did, you would need Julie as backup access to the Hawthorne fortune. Hence your recent romance. You played on her loneliness. It helped your efforts that she preferred to keep the affair quiet. Secrets, by their very nature, add intrigue and excitement."

"I'm not concerned about what you believe you know about me," Paulie-boy said. "But I am surprised you haven't addressed a very important point about the mushroom soup, namely that I ate it. I'm as much a victim as Holden or Harold."

Danny shook his head. "You checked yourself into the emergency room two hours after leaving the Hawthorne penthouse. Most of the soup was still in your stomach, undigested and easily expelled. You knew, from your research, that your chances of complete recovery were excellent."

"That's an outrageous accusation."

"You didn't call Holden until the following morning, Mr. Barnard. Why is that?"

Paulie-boy blinked, then said, "I called as soon as I was able."

Holden's mouth dropped even more. "You knew you were poisoned *hours* before you called me?"

"It wasn't like that."

"Then how was it?"

Danny said, "Mr. Hawthorne, the reason Mr. Barnard didn't call is that he did not want Harold to be warned. Simply put, he cared more about Harold dying than you living. Mr. Barnard may act like your friend, but most assuredly he is not. His interest has always been gaining access to and eventually controlling your father's fortune. You have always been a means to an end."

"I don't believe it," Holden said, his voice strained.

"Either before or after Mr. Barnard met you, he researched you. He learned that you and your sister would inherit a fortune. He determined that you were the more malleable, so he focused on you. He became your friend and arranged through you to meet your father. Perhaps he offered to back you up in a discussion you wanted to have with your father about a business idea, an idea you became excited about after Mr. Barnard carefully fed it to you. Perhaps Mr. Barnard knew the idea was bad and would be rejected by Harold. Perhaps, after the rejection, Mr. Barnard told you he'd be happy to talk with Harold privately and you agreed, grateful for your new friend's support, and Mr. Barnard used that opportunity to establish a relationship of his own with Harold. My guess is that Mr. Barnard and Harold came back to you and said that the idea had merit but that you and Mr. Barnard needed to do more work to vet it. My guess is that, after more time passed, the idea was allowed to quietly die."

The flush on Holden's cheek told me all I

needed to know about the accuracy of Danny's guesswork.

Danny continued, his focus still on Holden. "I suspect that, even as Mr. Barnard was using Harold, Harold was using Mr. Barnard to influence you. Your father wanted you to attend business school, so he conspired with Mr. Barnard to encourage you toward that decision. In other words, there was a reciprocity between Mr. Barnard and your father. Both parties knew and understood their roles."

Paulie-boy was shaking his head. "I don't recognize the person you're talking about."

"Bosh," Danny said, turning toward him. "At this point, your plan was unfolding flawlessly. You had Holden's friendship and were gaining Harold's trust. After years of trying and failing to persuade your startup clients to take you on as a founding legal partner, you'd managed to persuade the entrepreneurs at XerXes to do just that. You had Holden on board as a potential investor and were closing in on Harold. Then Claire entered the picture. You must have feared her potential to thwart your plans, a potential realized when Harold announced that most of his fortune would go to his foundation, controlled by her.

"After three years of assiduously developing a

relationship with Harold and working to gain his confidence, he'd cut you out. I don't know what tipped him off to your true nature — something small, probably, a look in your eyes, a careless conversational slip — but tipped off he undoubtedly was."

Paulie-boy shook his head, just barely. "This is nonsense."

"You're a careful planner, Mr. Barnard, resourceful and determined, which means you understand that the best response to a failed plan is a new plan. You knew you would need to act quickly, before the complicated legal work required to transfer ownership of a fortune from an individual to a foundation could be completed. The sooner you eliminated Harold and Claire, in other words, the sooner you could persuade Holden and Julie to challenge their father's plans and ensure the family fortune remained with them."

Paulie-boy pushed out his chair and stood. "I'm done here."

Holden jumped up, ready to rumble. "You're gonna sit back down, or I'll make you."

"Is that a threat?"

"A promise."

Paulie-boy looked around the room. "You all heard that."

"Sit down, Mr. Barnard," Danny said, weariness in his voice. "Mr. Hawthorne, calm yourself. Mr. Barnard doesn't want to leave. He has yet to hear the best part."

From his chair against the wall behind the two of them, Barry cleared his throat. "Sit down, Mr. Hawthorne."

Holden whipped around, startled. When he saw who was talking, he complied, trembling with anger and confusion.

Paulie-boy, meanwhile, stood there, tense from head to toe, weighing his next move. The lawyer part of his brain had to have noted that Danny's speculations didn't include a lick of evidence; he had to be counseling himself to get the hell out of the room before he made a mistake. At the same time, the risk-taking, ego-driven side of him had to be furious that his years of careful planning and hard work were being blown to hell by this smug blond giant. Even now, his ego had to be compelling him toward a counter-attack, even revenge.

Danny said, "You made a mistake, Mr. Barnard. A beginner's mistake. I'm sure you'll want to know what it was."

Paulie-boy smirked. "I'm going to sue you for slander when I leave this room." When Danny didn't reply, Paulie-boy shook his head and settled back into his seat.

On cue, the good Inspector Figueroa rose and dropped a piece of paper on the table in front of him. "This is a search warrant for your apartment, conducted yesterday morning, after you left for your morning workout at the gym."

Paulie-boy's face went beet-red. "This is outrageous," he said. "I wasn't even there. Warrants served on attorneys require special—"

"I'm fully aware of the law, Mr. Barnard," the inspector said. "We left a receipt."

"A receipt? You seized evidence? If your goons broke or damaged a single thing —"

Goons? The first real crack in Paulie-boy's emotional armor.

My turn. I stood up and dropped a second document on the table in front of him, where it landed with a satisfying slap.

"Crime lab report," I said. "Turns out the SFPD crime geeks aren't always slow or incompetent. Sometimes, with the right motivation, they can be pretty good. Especially when they know what they're looking for."

The report lay there on the table, aching to be read. At the top of the page was the "SFPD Forensic Laboratory" logo. Below that was the usual boilerplate — case number, investigating technician, date of report, and so on. And below that, spelled out in black and white in the box marked "Results," the good stuff. Paulie-boy didn't move a muscle, but he couldn't keep his eyes off the words typed on the page.

"What the report says," I announced to the room, "is that Paulie-boy here is one clean fellow. His place is nearly spotless — lick-the-floor clean. The kind of clean you get because you've scrubbed the heck out of it. The kind of clean you get because you know about the wonders of forensic science and want to guarantee that nobody ever finds a shred of evidence against you."

Barry's turn. He rose and stepped behind Paulie's chair.

Paulie blinked. His nostrils flared and he clenched one of his fists. He didn't move his head to look at Barry, but he sure as hell knew that Barry — big, bulky Barry — was standing mere inches behind him, motionless and ready. Physical presence like that is impossible to ignore. It does things to a fellow — ups the blood pressure, gets the adrenaline pumping. Even while the mind is trying desperately to keep calm, the body is preparing to flee or fight.

Barry cleared his throat. Then, using his Voice-of-God voice, he said, "You said *nearly* spotless."

"Paulie-boy missed a spot," I said. "Just a trace."

"Nonsense," Paulie-boy said, his voice strained and hoarse.

"It's all right here," I said. I scooted around the table, then leaned over Paulie-boy's shoulder and tapped my finger on the crime lab report. "I'm no geek, but it's right here."

Paulie-boy wanted to turn and tell me to stop crowding him, but the even stronger impulse was to focus on the words on the report in front of him.

Remorselessly, Danny piled on. "The only problem with your weapon of choice, Mr. Barnard, is that it isn't guaranteed to kill. Recovery is quite possible, even likely, when a small amount is ingested."

"This is insane."

"The lack of certainty troubled you, didn't it?" Danny said, ignoring him. "How much of a dose? That had to be vexatious. To maximize Harold Hawthorne's risk of death, you needed him to consume a sufficiently large helping."

Paul stared stone-faced at Danny, the mask of friendly affability long gone, not moving a muscle.

Danny leaned forward. "Which meant even the smallest details had to be attended to — details like uncooked mushrooms. Before you brought the lethal mushrooms to Harold's penthouse, you sautéed them in your kitchen. The last thing you wanted was for your careful planning to be ruined by Harold or Holden noticing uncooked mushrooms in their favorite soup."

Paul's lip twitched. Danny saw it and smiled, just for a second. "I'm sure you know where the police found the traces of *A. ocreata* in your apartment, Mr. Barnard. Would you care to explain where?"

"This is crazy," he said.

"In a place you didn't clean, Mr. Barnard."

"This is insane."

"Inside your oven vent."

From my spot at Paulie-boy's shoulder, I leaned over him again and flipped to the report's second page. "It's all there in the report," I said helpfully. "See, dumb ass? Right there."

"I am not a dumb ass!" he yelled, finally losing it. He rose abruptly and shoved me out of his way and tried to push past Barry.

"Ow," I said theatrically, holding my elbow. "He hurt me."

Inspector Figueroa tried to keep the smile off her face as she stepped up and said, "Paul Barnard, I'm placing you under arrest." Quickly, before he could blink, she grabbed his arms, slapped cuffs on him, and read him rights.

"For what?" he yelled. "You're crazy."

"For assault," she said.

"Ow," I said again.

"This is entrapment."

"Too bad about the poison in the vent," I shot back. "That isn't assault."

"I can explain that," he said before he could think.

And that, ladies and gentlemen, was what we'd been hoping for — what I call a magic moment, one of those oh-so-infrequent instances in which the universe decides to give instead of take away. Paulie-boy's excited utterance — made voluntarily, in front of multiple witnesses, after he'd been read his rights — was exactly what we so desperately needed.

It took Paulie-boy a few seconds, but he caught up. He looked at the crime lab report and search warrant on the table and then at me. "They're fake."

I took a bow. "Pleasure's all mine."

He snarled at me as Inspector Figueroa pushed him out the door.

Holden sat there, gaping. "What the hell just happened?"

"What happened, Mr. Hawthorne," Danny said,

"is that your father's killer just gave the police prob-able cause for a search warrant."

"How?"

"When he said he could explain the presence of *A. ocreata* residue in his vent hood, he admitted to its existence. Which means he also admitted lying to the police when he said he didn't have access to or knowledge of the murder weapon."

Julie pointed to the report on the table. "But the crime lab already told you that."

"No," Danny said, "the crime lab did not. The report on the table is a forgery. Courtesy of my associate, Mr. Sears."

"The report's a fake?" Holden said, still not getting it. "Why?"

"The report is a fake because no report exists," Danny said. "No report exists because no search of Mr. Barnard's apartment took place. No search occurred because no probable cause existed to justify it."

"Until now," Julie said.

"Correct," Danny said.

"Which means Claire didn't do it," Julie said, then turned to Claire. "You're innocent."

"I loved your father," Claire said, tears in her eyes.

Julie's eyes filled as well. "I'm sorry. For everything I've said and done. I shouldn't have said what I said about you — not about another woman. We put up with too much as it is. I hate when we turn on each other. We need to stick together."

"Thank you," Claire said, and I could tell she meant it.

CHAPTER
ELEVEN

ABOUT A MONTH AFTER THE TRIAL, Claire texted and asked to see us. When her gorgeous long legs sauntered into the bar, she found Barry and me in our usual spots. Next to us was Danny, who we'd dragged out of his house by threatening home invasion as the alternative.

Our former client was looking lovely and stress-free, her trademark combo of class and va-va-voom in full bloom. According to the media, her once-estranged daughter-in-law Julie was doing okay, too. She'd joined the board of her father's foundation, and she and Claire had shown up together at a recent society event acting like the friends it seemed they'd become. Holden was on the upswing as well — one of his small investments had hit it big, so people were starting to talk about him like he was some kind of visionary.

Since his conviction for murder, Paul Barnard had kept himself busy filing appeals.

Claire had a wrapped gift in her hands. "Gentlemen," she said. "I found this in Harold's wine cellar and thought of you."

"May I?" I said, reaching for it.

"Please."

Carefully, I removed the wrapping and unveiled a bottle of Midleton Dair Ghaelach, one of the finest whiskeys on the planet. With a low whistle, I aimed the label at Danny and Barry, then handed the bottle to Jimmy, who lined five shot glasses on the bar and, after a nod from Claire, poured.

Claire picked up her glass and held it in front of her. "A toast, to the four of you. And to my dad, for having the foresight to ask for your help."

With a murmur of agreement, we brought the whiskey to our lips. The taste, rich and creamy with a hint of oak, lingered on our tongues.

"Mrs. Hawthorne," Danny said after a suitable pause, "why don't you tell us why you're really here."

"I'm no longer your client," she said. "Call me Claire."

"Very well, Claire."

She looked at us, one by one, before returning her gaze to San Francisco's best detective.

I couldn't help but grin at the grimace that appeared on Danny's face when she said, "A friend of mine is in trouble and needs your help...."

THE END

SHOCK AND AWE
A SPECIAL EXPLOITS THRILLER

Catch a killer, save the world....

Lucy felt a jolt of shock — even horror — at the sight of Jack Ford, jerk extraordinaire, staring at her in surprise.

"You?" he said, anger flashing in his eyes.

Heat rushed to her cheeks. The humiliation — the betrayal — of their prior encounter came roaring back. Nausea surged through her.

Why had Special Exploits called them in?

What in the hell was going on?

On a billionaire's Mediterranean island, amidst a private gathering of the world's elite, a ruthless mastermind is selling a bio-weapon deadly enough to wipe out the human race.

Special Exploits agent Jack Ford and microbiologist Lucy Kimball, reluctant partners in a lethal game of catch-the-killer, must overcome their mutual loathing and learn to trust each other — if they hope to outplay a dangerous adversary whose bloody ambition knows no bounds….

Shock and Awe is an adrenaline-charged espionage thriller and a modern-day homage to classic spy adventure — packed with high-tech gadgets, propelled by desperate chases, and fueled by unlikely heroes battling unstoppable villains. Read at your peril….

Special Exploits Thrillers:

Shock and Awe (#1 — available now)

Bring It On (#2 — coming soon)

Do or Die (#3 — coming soon)

Get your copy now!

MICHAEL RYDER'S NEWSLETTER

Get an email update when a new Michael Ryder book is ready. You can unsubscribe at any time with one click.

Sign up at AuthorMichaelRyder.com

ABOUT THE AUTHOR

Michael Ryder's novels include *Never Trust Me* (a psychological thriller) and *Shock and Awe* (a spy thriller). His short stories have been published in *Compelling Science Fiction*, *Penumbra*, and *Fiction River*. After working as a journalist in Tokyo, New York, and Hong Kong, he moved to San Francisco and dove into technology and banking. Now a full-time purveyor of fiction, he's found most days in neighborhood cafes, typing madly into his trusty laptop.

AuthorMichaelRyder.com